lonely Leela and the new

# kindness chain

A STORY OF INSPIRATION..



WRITTEN AND ILLUSTRATED BY

SWATI JAIN

BlueRose ONE.com
Stories Matter
NewDelhi • London

**BLUEROSE PUBLISHERS**
India | U.K.



For permissions, requests or inquiries regarding this publication, please contact:

BLUEROSE PUBLISHERS
www.BlueRoseONE.com
info@bluerosepublishers.com
+91 8882 898 898
+4407342408967

ISBN: 978-93-7018-809-9

Cover Design: Swati Jain
Typesetting: Sagar

First Edition: June 2025

# Introduction

Swati is a fashion designer, Author and Artist

Studied in National institute of fashion design (NIFT Delhi) India. she is based in pune, India. she used to write stories in her holidays and she try to create something new related to sustainability to support NGOs, poor schools and orphanage.

This book Dedicated to my kids Vian and Valentina with best wishes and the big dreams inspired by all those bedtime stories we read together, when you were small.

My heartfelt thanks to my husband and family for encouraging me and BlueRose publishers for publishing my book of kindness.

**Thanks**

It was a bright morning at Lancer Elementary School. The bell rang, and the students hurried to their classrooms, excited to start the day.

Among them was Leela, a quiet, thoughtful girl who always sat in the back row. Leela always had a smile on her face even when no one noticed her.

She loved reading, drawing, and helping others. She was close to her classmates. Leela shared lunch and laugh at silly jokes with friends, but overtime, things changed.

Her best friend Sam joined a new group of friends. At first, Leela didn't mind. She thought that Sam was making new connections, but soon she noticed the distance growing.

Sam no longer holds a seat for Leela at lunch. Their inside jokes became old memories, and the worst of all was when Leela needed to talk but unfortunately , Sam was always too busy.

Leela felt lonely and was thinking... had she done something wrong? Was she not good enough? Another classmate began focusing on their own activities.

Slowly, Leela felt left out during recess. Leela often sat on the bench near the playground, watching the other kids laughing and playing.

She wished someone would notice her, but as the days passed, they were too busy with their own games to realize Leela was alone.

Leela was a very courageous and brave girl. The lonely bench hurt, but instead of dwelling on it, she decided to focus on something she had always loved, which was drawing and art.

At first, it was just a way to pass the time, but later, as days turned into weeks, she realised something... that drawing was not just a distraction.

It was her escape, her peace, and most of all, her strength. She poured her emotions into her art.

**In her society *drawing* competition, she *also* *won a first prize.***

One day, the class received a special project. The teacher, Mrs. Bakshi asked them to create a “kindness chain”. It was a group project.

*Kids need to write and paint about a kindness chain project Leela, Kelvin, and Sam, the most popular kids in class, were in the same group.*

Kelvin and Sam whispered about Leela that she never talks.

**As they started the project, Leela hesitated at first, unsure of what to write and paint but then later, Leela surprised them.**

She had amazing ideas, her drawings were incredible, and she even helped solve a problem her group was stuck on.

All groups started working on an act of kindness chain.

Later, kids saw Leela was really smart at her work. Everyone admitted and appreciated her for her amazing drawings. Leela smiled and said, “Thanks” to everyone.

The next day at recess, Kelvin approached Leela, he noticed Leela sitting alone during recess, he included Leela in the game. and also, Sam called her over.

"Hey, Leela. Do you want to play with us?"

Leela's heart warmed. Maybe she wasn't invisible after all.

The next day, Kelvin asked Leela again during recess,"Hey, Leela," he said. "There is a new girl Eva who wants to join us in an act of kindness. Can we include her.". This shows how dedicatedly and honestly Leela's group is working on the kindness chain.

Leela's face lit up with joy. "Really??? I would love to !" As they played, other classmates began to notice how fun and friendly Leela was.

They realized they had been so focused on their own lives that they forgot to look around and care for everyone in their class.

Kids decided to do something kind; like at lunch time, Sam dropped her crayons all over the floor. Kelvin helped her to pick them up.

Sam said thanks to Kelvin for help. Other students in the class also started helping each other and spreading kindness. Kelvin, feeling extra cheerful, decided to keep the kindness going.

From that day on, Leela's lonely bench became a gathering spot, where no one sat alone for long.

A small action of kindness can inspire others and make the whole world a better place.

Moral of the story: Just because someone is quiet doesn't mean they should be ignored. Everyone deserves to be seen. Everyone should take the first step to include all.

Kindmess Grows Herre

The class learned an important lesson: friends might see Leela no longer sit alone and the kindness chain grew longer, each Link a reminder of how small acts of care could make a big difference.

This smallest act of kindness could brighten someone's day.

Kindness is giving hope to those who think they are alone in this world...